Katie Woo's

❋ Neighborhood ❋

Super Paramedic!

NO LONGER PROPERTY OF
ANYTHINK LIBRARIES /
RANGEVIEW LIBRARY DISTRICT

by Fran Manushkin

illustrated by Laura Zarrin

D0027778

PICTURE WINDOW BOOKS
a capstone imprint

Katie Woo's Neighborhood is published by Picture Window Books,
A Capstone Imprint
1710 Roe Crest Drive
North Mankato, Minnesota 56003
www.capstonepub.com

Text © 2020 Fran Manushkin
Illustrations © 2020 Picture Window Books

All rights reserved. No part of this publication may be reproduced in
whole or in part, or stored in a retrieval system, or transmitted in any
form or by any means, electronic, mechanical, photocopying, recording,
or otherwise, without written permission of the publisher.

Library of Congress Cataloging-in-Publication Data
Names: Manushkin, Fran, author. | Zarrin, Laura, illustrator.
Title: Super paramedic! / by Fran Manushkin ; illustrated by
    Laura Zarrin.
Description: North Mankato, Minnesota : Picture Window Books, [2019] |
    Series: Katie Woo's neighborhood | Summary: When Katie's
    grandmother trips and breaks her ankle, Katie learns about the
    importance of paramedics to her neighborhood.
Identifiers: LCCN 2019005850| ISBN 9781515844563 (hardcover) |
    ISBN 9781515845577 (pbk.) | ISBN 9781515844600 (ebook pdf)
Subjects: LCSH: Woo, Katie (Fictitious character)—Juvenile fiction. |
    Chinese Americans—Juvenile fiction. | Emergency medical
    technicians—Juvenile fiction. | Emergency medical services—Juvenile
    fiction. | Grandmothers--Juvenile fiction. | CYAC: Chinese Americans—
    Fiction. | Emergency medical technicians—Fiction. | Grandmothers—
    Fiction.
Classification: LCC PZ7.M3195 Su 2019 | DDC 813.54 [E]—dc23
LC record available at https://lccn.loc.gov/2019005850

Graphic Designer: Bobbie Nuytten

Printed and bound in the USA.
PA71

Table of Contents

Katie's Neighborhood

Police

Library

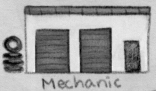
Mechanic

City
Hall

Grocery Store

Post Office

Chapter 1
Oh No!

Katie and her grandma

were having lunch.

"I love your new bracelet,"

said Katie.

"Me too!" said Grandma.

"Hearts are the best."

After lunch, Grandma
was ready to go home.

Katie said, "I'll walk you
to your car."

Whoosh! Haley O'Hara

came skating by with her

brothers and sisters.

"Hi!" yelled Katie.

"Hi!" yelled Haley.

Grandma told Katie,

"My car is at the end of

the block."

They had almost reached

the car, when—

Grandma tripped on a broken sidewalk!

She fell down—hard!

"I hurt my foot," said

Grandma. "I can't move it."

Katie wanted to cry, but

she stayed calm.

"I'll go get Mom," she said.

Katie's mom called 911.

She told Grandma, "The paramedics will be here soon. They will help you."

"I hope so," said Katie.

Haley O'Hara said,

"Put my sweater on your

grandma. She should keep

warm until the ambulance

comes."

"How do you know that?"

asked Katie.

"My family is always

breaking something,"

said Haley. "I have lots of

practice."

Chapter 2

Help Is on the Way

Soon they heard the loud

siren. The paramedics were

there!

Katie was so happy to

see them.

One paramedic listened
to Grandma's heart.

The other one examined
Grandma's foot.

"Your heart is fine," said

one of the paramedics. "But

I think your ankle is broken.

We need to take you to the

hospital."

The paramedics lifted
Grandma into the ambulance.
They were gentle and strong.
Katie and her mom drove
to the hospital.

At the hospital, a doctor put a cast on Grandma's foot. She told her, "After six weeks you will be fine."

Grandma smiled. "Thank you! I want to thank the paramedics too."

But they had rushed to another accident.

Chapter 3

Thank You, Paramedics!

Katie said, "Grandma,

I'm glad you will get better.

But I am sad that you lost

your new bracelet. It's gone!"

But it wasn't! When Katie got home, Haley was waiting.

"Here is your grandma's bracelet. I found it in the grass."

Katie hugged Haley. "You're

the best!"

Then she called Grandma.

"Haley found your bracelet!"

"Terrific!" said Grandma.

"There is one more thing
I want to do," said Katie.
She got out her paper
and paints.

Katie began to write and
draw.

"Hearts are the best,"
Katie said. She drew a lot
of them.

Dear Paramedics,
thank you so much
for helping my
grandma. You
are SUPER!

Love,
Katie

Glossary

accident (AK-si-duhunt)—an unfortunate and unplanned event

ambulance (AM-byuh-luhnss)—a vehicle that takes sick or injured people to the hospital

ankle (ANG-kuhl)—the joint that connects your foot to your leg

cast (KAST)—a hard plaster covering that supports a broken arm or leg

examined (eg-ZAM-uhnd)—looked over carefully

paramedic (pa-ruh-MED-ik)—a specially trained person who provides a range of emergency medical care before or during transport to a hospital

siren (SYE-ruhn)—a device that makes a loud, shrill sound

Katie's Questions

1. What traits make a good paramedic? Would you like to be a paramedic? Why or why not?

2. Compare paramedics to doctors. How are they the same? How are they different?

3. Katie's grandma had a medical emergency. There are important steps to take when someone has this sort of emergency. Thinking about the story, can you list the steps?

4. The title of this book is *Super Paramedic!* How is a paramedic like a superhero?

5. Katie writes a thank-you note to the two paramedics who helped her grandma. Write a thank-you note to someone who has helped you.

Katie Interviews a Paramedic

Katie: Hello, Ms. Thomas. Thanks so much for meeting with me so I can learn about being a paramedic! What's the best thing about your job?

Ms. Thomas: There are lots of great things about being a paramedic. The ambulance is really cool, and every day is different because the patients are always different. But the best thing about my job is that I get to help people every day.

Katie: You helped my grandma, that's for sure! Do a lot of the people you help have broken bones like Grandma?

Ms. Thomas: Sure, but the most common things we find are heart and breathing problems. Even when a patient has fallen, we listen to their heart and lungs with a stethoscope. We also check to see how fast their heart is beating and make sure their blood pressure is okay.

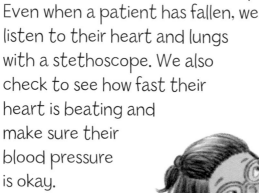

Katie: You do a lot of important work! How long did you have to go to school to become a paramedic?

Ms. Thomas: First I studied to be an EMT (emergency medical technician), which took six months. Then I went on to become a paramedic. That was another year of classes, plus a few months of practice hours. After all that, I had to take a special test to become an official paramedic. I have to retake that test every two years too.

Katie: Last question . . . do you ever drive the ambulance?

Ms. Thomas: Usually my partner drives. He's an EMT. Since I have a bit more medical training, I work with the patients while he speeds us to the hospital. But sometimes I do drive. Did you know ambulances have special machines that turn traffic lights green? We can drive straight to the patient or hospital without stopping.

Katie: Thanks again for talking to me today, Ms. Thomas!

Ms. Thomas: You're welcome, Katie! It was my pleasure.

About the Author

Fran Manushkin is the author of Katie Woo, the highly acclaimed, fan-favorite early reader series, as well as the popular Pedro series. Her other books include *Happy in Our Skin*, *Baby, Come Out!* and the best-selling board books *Big Girl Panties* and *Big Boy Underpants*. There is a real Katie Woo: Fran's great-niece, who doesn't get into trouble like the Katie in the books. Fran lives in New York City, three blocks from Central Park, where she can often be found bird-watching and daydreaming. She writes at her dining room table, without the help of her two naughty cats, Chaim and Goldy.

About the Illustrator

Laura Zarrin spent her early childhood in the St. Louis, Missouri, area. There she explored creeks, woods, and attic closets, climbed trees, and dug for artifacts in the backyard, all in preparation for her future career as an archeologist. She never became one, however, because she realized she's much happier drawing in the comfort of her own home while watching TV. When she was twelve, her family moved to the Silicon Valley in California, where she still resides with her very logical husband and teen sons, and their illogical dog, Cody.